Flowers *for all* Seasons

MARGARET PEIFFER

Order this book online at www.trafford.com
or email orders@trafford.com

Most Trafford titles are also available at major online book retailers.

 www.trafford.com

North America & international
toll-free: 844 688 6899 (USA & Canada)
fax: 812 355 4082

Our mission is to efficiently provide the world's finest, most comprehensive book publishing
service, enabling every author to experience success. To find out how to publish your book,
your way, and have it available worldwide, visit us online at www.trafford.com

ISBN: 978-1-6987-0573-6 (sc)
ISBN: 978-1-6987-0572-9 (e)

Library of Congress Control Number: 2021902141

Print information available on the last page.

Trafford rev. 02/09/2021

Flowers *for all* Seasons

To individuals who
recognize the beauty and peace
flowers bring to our environment.
No matter the season or the celebration
flowers show off their beauty to bring
a message of hope and healing.

Where flowers bloom, so does hope.

March 15. 2020

"Beginning today, there will be no lessons in the school building. Learning will take place at home guided by your teacher and your parents on the computer."

Ten-year old African American twins, Jane and Joseph, were confused about the "distance learning" described by the reporter.

A contagious virus was spreading throughout the world. Groups were forbidden to meet. This included church services, schools, libraries, sports, fitness centers, parks, restaurants, movies, and all stores except grocery stores, pharmacies, and gas stations. At all times families would be quarantined in their homes except to buy groceries, medicine, and gas. Everyone had to wear masks to cover their nose and mouth when in public. Frequent hand-washing was imposed, and people had to stand or sit six feet from one another in public.

Many people would suffer and die as a result of the virus. There was no cure. Doctors and nurses worked long hours in hospitals to try to save the sick people.

This was the first time the twins heard the word "quarantine". Joseph read the definition from the dictionary," quarantine means a restraint on the movement of persons to prevent the spread of disease". "Distance learning" and "pandemic" were not yet part of their vocabulary.

Mom and dad sat down with the twins to explain the seriousness of the situation. The twin's joy of no school turned to alarm about their grades and not seeing their friends.

Suddenly their home was not a happy place to be. For several months they would be expected to use the computer to do assignments directed by their teacher, Mrs. Henderson. They would follow a schedule of subjects as if they were at school, but their desks would be the dining room table.

At first it was fun. They carefully placed their school supplies on the book shelf so they would be handy on "school days". Snacks and lunch broke up the monotony of the day. Mom was there to settle any arguments.

The newness of the situation wore off after the first week. There were arguments over who was finished first, who had the right answers, and who had the neatest paper. Even though they were in the same grade at school and did the same assignments, sibling rivalry was part of all assignments at the dining room table.

Mom decided to have a meeting with the family to mediate relationships and put the twin's energy to work after they finished their assignments. They liked nature so they settled on a nature project. Growing flowers would be interesting.

This project would require planning, research, getting to know the flowers of each season, and learning the symbolism of the flowers. The twins remembered a poster in their classroom.

Bloom where

you are planted.

The twins thought their project would bring the poster to life. The plan was almost complete. Jane asked, "Who can we share our project with? Dad takes care of our flowers."

Two elderly ladies, Lucy and Linda, lived next door. They weren't friendly with their colored neighbors. They didn't return the friendly gestures of neighbors. They kept the ball that accidentally landed in the ladies' back yard. The twins thought it was time for a change.

The twins noticed the ladies had small patches of soil near their back porch where they sat every afternoon if the weather was pleasant. The twins planned to visit the ladies and explain the project.

The ladies were surprised when the twins knocked on the door. Lucy invited them in. Joseph explained the purpose of the visit. The ladies were happy to hear about their gift. In return the ladies would help the twins with their assignments if needed. They, too, loved flowers. They, too, would value the friendship of the twins and their family.

Lucy served the twins lemonade and delicious chocolate chip cookies. A bond of friendship was woven that day.

Over the next several months, the ladies explained the Civil Rights Movement, the marches, protests, and the reasons for changes. Jane wept when the ladies told about African Americans being denied a library card. Colored people could not use the restrooms, waiting rooms, or restaurants of white people.

The twins had a place to plant flowers. Where could they purchase the bulbs and seeds? The twins remembered Jesus did not ask impossible things of His people. He would provide a way to serve others since He was asking the twins to serve God by serving their neighbors.

They couldn't go to Home Depot because garden supplies were not considered necessary during this period of quarantine. Food, medicine, and gas were necessary; flowers were not.

Dad remembered he had some seeds and some bulbs left over from last year in the garage. One problem was already solved. The bulbs, however, would have to wait to bloom next year because they must be planted in the fall. They are dormant in the winter months. Flowers that bloom from seeds can be planted in the spring and summer.

It was fun learning and discussing flowers with Lucy and Linda. They seemed to enjoy the company of the youngsters as they excitedly outlined their plans. Dad helped the twins chart facts about flowers that beautify each season.

The twins did their assignments before working on their gardening project. They completed their household chores also.

The following chart outlines the master plan for the garden. The chart includes only a few of the flowers of each season.

MASTER PLAN

Spring	March, April May	Crocuses, Daffodils, Tulips,	Bulbs	Perennials
Summer	June, July August	Impatiens, Petunias, Roses, Pansies	Seeds	Annuals
Fall	September, October, November	Sunflowers, Chrysanthemums (mums)	Seeds	Annuals
Winter	December, January, February	Poinsettias	Seeds	Annuals

These charts present some additional facts about the flowers to be planted by the twins. They will make for interesting conversations with Lucy and Linda.

SPRING	
Crocus	Used by the Greeks for wreaths for the head. Symbolizes youthfulness and cheerfulness. 
Daffodil	Symbolizes rebirth and new beginnings. Is a life-affirming, bright, joyful, and yellow color. 

Tulip	Present many beautiful, radiant colors on strong, sturdy stems. Symbolizes perfect love.

SUMMER

Impatiens	Called Busy Lizzies and Touch-Me-Nots. Like moist soil and gives the gardener bright colors.

Petunia	Is a trumpet-shaped flower. Have single or double blooms, ruffled, smooth, veined, striped petals.

Rose	Symbolizes love, gratitude, purity, and innocence. Has 37 classes. Outstanding beauty.

Pansy	These purple and yellow flowers endure the chill of fall and the bitter cold of winter.

FALL

Sunflower	Symbolizes adoration, loyalty, and longevity. Center seeds are used for snacking.

Mums	Symbolize happiness, love, longevity, and joy. Has a long name chrysanthemum shortened to mum.

WINTER

Poinsettia	Symbolizes good cheer, success, and celebration. Have colors of red, pink, and white. Christmas joy is their message at the birth of Jesus in December. These flowers cannot grow where there is snow. They grow in glass houses and require special care when snow blankets the earth.

These flowering bushes and trees present their beauty and show that the summer season is coming soon.

Forsythia bushes	Small yellow flowers burst out on a bush to proclaim springtime is here.
Dogwood trees	Produce white flowers that symbolize the events of Holy Week – the week before Easter.
Cherry trees	Spring calls everyone to take in the beauty of the pink and white blossoms that symbolize friendship.

Forsythia bushes spread their branches filled with small yellow flowers to brighten yards and gardens. Each year they sprout their tiny flowers as if to say,

"Winter is over;

Put your coats and boots away.

Put a happy smile on your face.

And come outside and play."

Dogwood trees are symbolic of the Lenten season. Its white petals are shaped in the form of a cross and tipped in red as a reminder of the blood shed by Jesus on the cross. In the sorrows of Holy Week, Jesus completed the work He was sent to do. The dogwood tree blossoms are a gentle reminder of how much love it took to save a world.

Each year cherry blossom trees attract thousands of people to gaze at their beauty. The trees surround the Tidal Basin in Washington, D.C. The first 2,000 trees were a gift from Japan in 1910.

However, these trees had to be destroyed because they were diseased. The gift was renewed in 1912 with over 3 thousand trees because of the growing friendship between the two countries. In 1965, another 3,800 trees made their way to American shores.

They are not fruit-bearing trees and branches or flowers are not to be touched for fear the tender pink flowers wither and die. Nature displays her glory for all to see. Tourists and those who live close by in Maryland and Virginia thank the Creator for such breathtaking beauty.

There are some holidays when flowers take center stage. The chart below outlines these holidays.

January 1	New Year's Day	New beginnings
Jan.3rd Mon.	Martin L. King	Leader of civil rights
February 14	Valentine's Day	Messages of love
February 12/22	Washington/Lincoln	Happy birthday to Presidents
May 2nd Sun.	Mother's Day	Honor and thank mothers
May 31	Memorial Day	Veterans who served in war
June 2nd Sun.	Father's Day	Honor and thank fathers
July 4	World peace	End of World War II in 1945
Sept. 1st Mon.	Labor Day	Celebrate all workers
Nov. 4th Thurs.	Thanksgiving Day	Special thanks for everything
December 25	Birth of Jesus	Savior of the world

The meaning of flowers or flora is symbolism. No one flower means family, nor does any flower have just one definition. Rather they are a collection of thoughts, ideas and symbols for things that remind us of a family such as love, children, home, and life. One chooses flowers symbolizing life, relationship, and caring.

Flowers are used to celebrate and honor relatives, friends, and neighbors. At Christmas and Easter, the altars in churches are adorned with flowers to remind us of the beauty of Jesus' life and His resurrection from the dead after the sad events of Good Friday. There is no better gift than flowers to celebrate happy events such as weddings, the birth of a baby, and graduation.

Flowers help to cheer a friend who is sick. At funerals and memorial services, flowers express God's love for the person who has met his or her creator. On special days through the year, we honor those who work or have died in defense of our country.

'The following are some trivia facts about some of the flowers featured in the project. See if you can find out more about the flowers and write your findings in the space below.

Petunias – They love to spread their charm amidst other flowers in the garden and in pots that decorate doorways and porches. There are many varieties of these popular flowers. They love to be outside, so they are not suited for bouquets.

Sunflowers – They are large, tall flowers that annually burst forth with bright yellow petals and brown centers. They symbolize the harvest of vegetables. They are evident of the fall season.

<u>Chrysanthemums</u> – These flowers blend in nicely with the leaves that are beginning to show colors of orange, red, yellow, and rust. Their cultivation began in Japan during the 8th-12th centuries. The people of Japan hold festivals each fall to recognize their beauty just as the people of America hold festivals in spring to recognize the cherry blossoms.

<u>Poinsettias</u> – These flowers herald the joys of Christmas. Joel Roberto Poinsett, the first American Ambassador to Mexico and a Congressman, is credited as the first person to introduce poinsettias to America after discovering them in Mexico. The main attraction is its red, pink, and white leaves, not its flowers. The flowers are the yellow clusters in the center of the leaves.

It took some time in April and May to clear the spaces for planting flowers. Dad showed the twins how to prepare the soil for the seeds. Before the seeds began to grow, the twins researched pictures of the flowers and conversations centered on their beauty and why we use them at celebrations. They would have to wait several weeks to see the result of their work.

So ends our story of flowers and friendship. The ladies no longer felt isolated in the community. When small groups got together for a picnic, they invited Lucy and Linda to join the gathering. A book club helped to fill the lonely days and strengthen the bonds of friendship.

The ladies helped Jane and Joseph with difficult history, math, and English lessons. The twins learned how to chart information so that analysis and differences could be easily learned. The ladies' careers as teachers helped other children in the community. The ladies no longer felt isolated because their skills as teachers were still useful. Families were thankful for the ladies' offer of help. When the ball landed in the ladies' yard, the ladies threw it back instead of keeping it.

There are many other resources that provide knowledge about flowers if you are interested. This book is the beginning of your search for God's beautiful decoration of the earth. The Botanical Gardens in Washington, D.C. feature all kinds of plants and flowers. They are cared for by botanists who have studied plants and flowers so they can answer the questions of visitors and students.

Kindness to their neighbors made a definite effect on Jane and Joseph. Imitate them and your life will be blessed!

Happiness
blooms
within this
community.

Glossary

This story contains words that may not be familiar to you. This glossary expands your vocabulary on the topic of flowers.

annuals	flowers that must be replanted each year (for example: petunias)
botany	the discovery and sharing of knowledge about plants and flowers and their environment in order to preserve and enrich life
bulb	thick, round root of a plant that is under ground (for example: tulips and crocuses)
dormant	not actively growing
enhance	improve
longevity	length of life
mediate	to bring order to a dispute
pandemic	wide spread outbreak of disease
perennials	plants that bloom from year to year
sprout	when plants push through the soil

The author has written and published six books for children at various ages. Words appeal to her, and she wants children to value them too. She valued correct words in her work on her Bachelor of Business Administration at George Washington University and in her public speaking opportunities. After retiring from the government in 1997, she worked with special needs children who needed help with their reading. She also worked with ESL adults who wanted to improve their English language skills.

Jane and Joseph, twins, find themselves in the midst of a pandemic with strict limitations on who they could communicate with and where they could go. They found an outlet for their interest and energy by befriending two elderly ladies. The twins were interested in science and decided to research and plant flowers and discuss seasonal flowers and their symbolism. In return, the ladies, retired teachers, helped them with their assignments.

Printed in the United States
By Bookmasters